The
LITTLE BLUE TUK-TUK

First published in Thailand by Thai Watana Panich Press, 2000
Second edition printed by Sirivatana Interprint Public Co. Ltd., Bangkok, 2006
This edition printed by Sirivatana Interprint Public Co. Ltd., Bangkok, 2010

Sirivatana Interprint Public Company Limited
Bangkok Thailand

The Little Blue Tuk-tuk

Janice Santikarn
Illustrated by Sukit Tanmankong

The little blue tuk-tuk was rolling along the streets of Bangkok grinning from ear to ear. He was a brand-new taxi and how handsome he thought he looked: with his sparkling blue coat; his bouncy red seats and long, coloured ribbons flapping in the breeze.

But what he loved best was his "Taxi" sign for he had always dreamed of having people sitting in his back seat, smiling as he took them for a ride

Suddenly a hand waved out to him and his engine roared with excitement, "**brroomm, brroom-brroom, brooom**". He had spotted his first customers.

They were five noisy schoolboys who scrambled up into the tiny back seat before the tuk-tuk sped off again - with arms and legs and bags still hanging over his sides.

As he raced away, the little tuk-tuk shouted, "Hey, everyone, look at me! It's just like I always dreamed!" But then all of a sudden his back seat shook and he began wobbling from side to side.

It was the schoolboys; they were laughing and pushing each other, rocking the little tuk-tuk back and forth, and almost tipping him over. "*Eeeeerrrr,*" he cried, "I don't like this at *aaaall.*" Nobody ever told me that being a taxi could be so *scaaary!*"

When the boys finally got out, he let out a huge sigh, "Pheeewwww!", and pulled over to rest outside a marketplace. There he found his next customer; an old woman with two huge shopping baskets crammed to the top with fruit.

"Aaaah, this is more like it," he thought. "A sweet old lady; there's nothing scary about her!"

So off they went, happily winding through the streets, until …
"boing-boing!", *"boing-boing!"* … his tyres hit a bump in the road and he bounced up into the air. Then … *"boing!"*, *"boing!"* … the little old lady bounced up too. And …*"boing-boing!"*, *"boing-boing-boing!"* … the pieces of fruit bounced up out of their baskets and flew out onto the street. Split! Splat! Ooooh, yuck! Seeds, peels and juice lay splattered across the road.

"Stop, stop!" screamed the old lady, pounding on the tuk-tuk's seats. "Let me out right now!"

Angrily, she climbed down and shook her fist at the driver. "Just look what you've done to my fruit! I'm *not* paying for *that* ride!"

As he watched her stomp away, the poor little tuk-tuk moaned. "*Oh, nooo!*" Maybe being a Taxi wasn't such a good idea after all."

Then he noticed a small boy and his mother waiting by the side of the road. "They look nice and friendly. I'm sure this ride will be more fun."

9

But just after they climbed in, something strange began to happen. His little body felt cold and his back seat was wet and soggy. "*Brrrr!*" he shivered. "What's happening to me?"

Peeking into his mirror he spied the little boy licking a chocolate ice cream. Gooey brown globs were oozing over his hands and dripping onto the seat.

"*Brrrrr!*" he shivered again. Then he started to sneeze, "AH"…
"AAAH"… "AAAHHH…TCHOOO!" And he shot into the air, crashing
to the ground, and knocking the whole ice cream cone onto his floor.

Now he was even colder and he let out a thunderous sneeze, "AAAAAAAATTTCCHHOOOOOOOO!" which blew his engine apart and he couldn't go any further.

"Oh, no," groaned the driver. "If the tuk-tuk doesn't run, I won't make any money to feed my family". So he quickly set to work, hammering and cutting and welding, and by early next morning the little blue tuk-tuk was back on the road again.

Right away he spotted some tourists waiting for a ride. "Aaah," he grinned. "I've never met any foreigners before. This should be exciting."

But it wasn't exciting *at all!* The tourists were big and heavy, not like the little old lady he had carried the day before.

Driving them around the city sights, he soon grew hot and tired. His engine whined, his seats sagged and his blue coat filled with sweat.

Hour after hour, he drove his passengers to temples, museums and palaces. And hour after hour they climbed in and out of his back seat, as they wandered off to take photos, and left him waiting in the sun.

By late afternoon, the little tuk-tuk's wheels could hardly turn. His body dragged, his eyelids drooped and all three tyres were aching. Finally, when he came to his next stop, he waited until the tourists were out of sight, and then he crawled away to rest under the large, shady leaves of a nearby tree.

When the man and woman returned, they found him fast asleep. "ZZZZZZZZ!", "ZZZZZZZZZZZ!", "ZZZZZZ!" Frantically the driver shook him. "Please, *pleeeeaaassseee* wake up!" But the little blue tuk-tuk just kept right on snoring, "ZZZZZZZZ!", "ZZZZZZZZ!", "ZZZZZZZZZ!"

Finally the driver threw up his hands. "That's it! This tuk-tuk has got to go! I need a taxi that will work all day, not one that sleeps when it gets hot or breaks down when it feels cold."

So the little blue tuk-tuk was sold. But it wasn't long before he caused his new owner trouble too, and he was sold once more...then again...and again, until at last he refused to run at all.

No matter how many people tried, no one could start his engine and no one could get him to move. So the little blue tuk-tuk was scrapped; he was thrown onto a garbage heap and left there all alone.

Day after day and night after night he sat at the top of that heap. In the hot season the sun beat down, melting his rubber tyres and burning his glossy blue coat.

When it was wet, the pouring rains soaked right through his seats. The bouncy red cushions tore open and clumps of stuffing spilled out. His roof sagged and the colours ran from his ribbons, which now hung by his side hardly moving at all.

But the saddest thing was his "Taxi" sign. It was cracked and covered with mud and when the little blue tuk-tuk looked up at it he began to cry. Somehow he knew he would never drive through the streets as a taxi again.

As the weeks dragged by the little blue tuk-tuk grew more sad and lonely. Then one morning he heard the sound of children laughing far off in the distance. As he listened, the sound drew closer and closer until all of a sudden three boys appeared at the top of the garbage pile.

At first the little tuk-tuk let out a cheer. "Hooray, at last I have someone to talk to!" But then he remembered...he wasn't a shiny blue tuk-tuk anymore, he was just an old piece of junk. Quickly he lowered his headlights and hoped that the children wouldn't notice him.

But they *did* see him. And they didn't mind that he was dirty and tattered and torn. Instead, they climbed up into his seats and played with him for hours.

To the tuk-tuk's surprise, the boys came back the very next day and the next day after that and he was the happiest he had been in a long, long time.

Then one day something unusual happened. The children brought a man along with them. "Hmm, what's he doing here?" the little taxi wondered. "I'm sure he hasn't come to play."

And he was right – for the man began circling slowly around the tuk-tuk's body, inspecting the broken seats, his dirty blue coat and ribbons and his muddy "Taxi" sign.

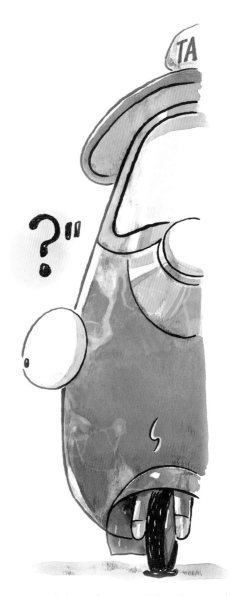

When he had finished, the man stood back, nodded to the children, and smiled. "Uh oh," thought the tuk-tuk, "What they are planning to do?"

28

The next morning the man returned with two workmen who were driving a big truck. They lifted the little tuk-tuk onto the back of it then drove him away to a garage behind the man's house.

Then, before he knew what was happening, the two men began tearing him apart. They yanked out his seats, tore off his ribbons, pulled out his engine, and even his "*Taxi*" sign too. "*Aaagh!*" he shrieked. "What are they doing to me?"

Then suddenly the men grabbed him again. "Splash, rub, ting, ping!" He could hardly believe his eyes. He was just like new! Polished and painted, with brand-new seats and ribbons, and even a gleaming Taxi sign on top. "Chaiyo!*" he shouted. "I'm a Taxi again!"... Or was he? For he still had one part missing – his engine.

* Chaiyo is a Thai word which means "hooray".

But before he could worry about that, the two men lifted him up and carried him away into a large room. It had huge glass windows all around and a view of the street outside. "Where am I now?" he wondered. "Is this a showroom? Am I going to be sold again?"

However, when he looked around more closely, he saw he wasn't in a showroom; it was some kind of shop - and everything inside it was made in Thailand. There were colourful silk clothes; big pots and vases; necklaces of shells and pearls; and sparkling rubies and sapphires.

He scratched his head. "Why did they put me in here amongst all these beautiful things? I'm just a little blue tuk-tuk, I don't belong with them."

Then he heard a voice say, "Come with me; this way". It was the man he had seen at the rubbish dump. He was talking with two customers and they were walking right towards him. "Oh, dear," he worried. "Now what?"

33

He watched nervously while the customers bought a ticket and then climbed up into his back seat. "This is *silly*," he scoffed. "How can I take them for a ride? I'm stuck in the middle of a shop and I don't even have an *engine* ."

Just as he said that, the customers began to smile. Then suddenly the man pulled out a camera and "Snap!" he took their picture. "So that's it!" the tuk-tuk shouted. "I'm not a taxi anymore, I'm a tourist attraction! People pay money to have their photos taken with me."

A huge grin filled his face and it stayed there all day long as customers kept on coming; one after another, sitting in his back seat, smiling, and having their photos taken.

And when a little girl climbed up onto his back seat, he smiled the biggest smile you've ever seen...stretching from one headlight all the way across to the other...for he knew his dream had finally come true!

MEET THE AUTHOR

I am Australian and have lived in Thailand for over 20 years. I am married to a Thai and have three children. When I'm not writing you can find me on the golf course or visiting with students at various schools in the region. This is one of many books I've written about Thailand. I hope you enjoy it.

OTHER BOOKS BY THE SAME AUTHOR

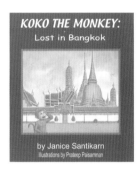

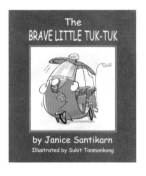

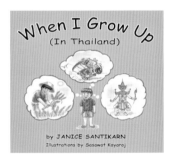

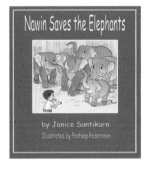

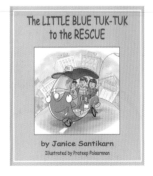